The Friendly Beasts

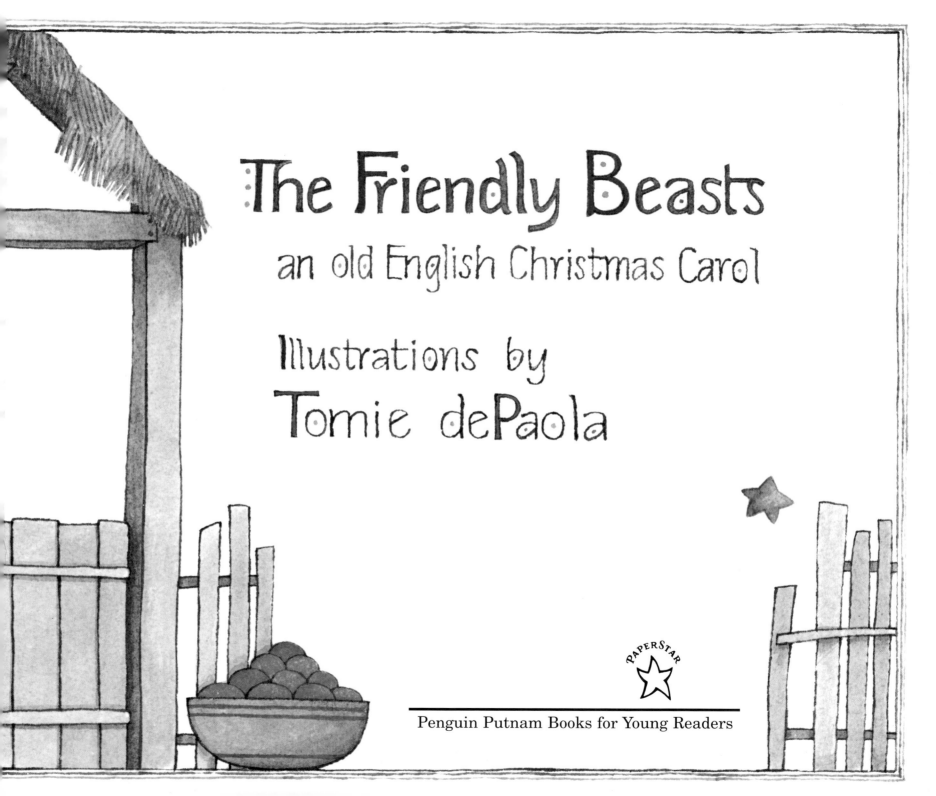

The Friendly Beasts

an old English Christmas Carol

Illustrations by

Tomie dePaola

Penguin Putnam Books for Young Readers

A PaperStar Book, published in 1998 by Penguin Putnam Books for Young Readers,
345 Hudson Street, New York, NY 10014. PaperStar is a registered trademark
of The Putnam Berkley Group, Inc. The PaperStar logo is a trademark of
The Putnam Berkley Group, Inc. Originally published in 1981 by G. P. Putnam's Sons.
Published simultaneously in Canada. Manufactured in China.
Library of Congress Cataloging-in-Publication Data
Main entry under title:
The Friendly beasts.
Summary: In this old English Christmas carol the friendly stable
beasts tell of the gifts they have given to the newborn Jesus.
[1. Carols, English.   2. Christmas music.   3. Folk songs, English]   I. DePaola, Tomie.
PZ8.3.F9118   783.6'5   80-15391
ISBN 978-0-698-11661-0
9   10   8

for Wolfgang and Hanni

Jesus our brother, strong and good,
Was humbly born in a stable rude;
And the friendly beasts around Him stood,
Jesus our brother, strong and good.

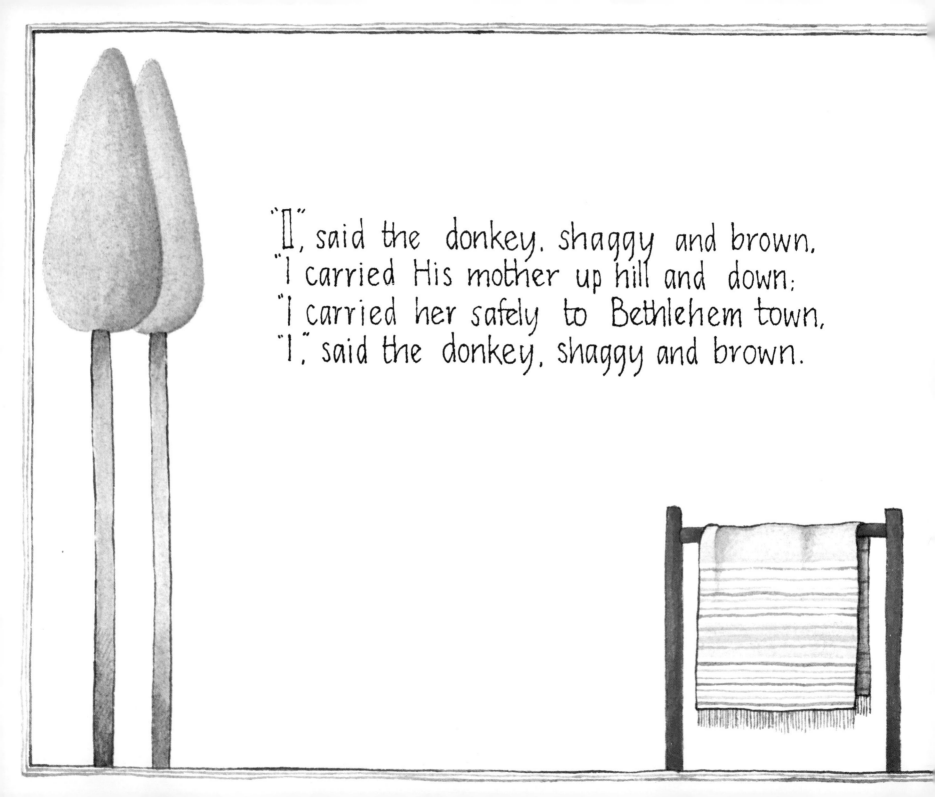

"I", said the donkey, shaggy and brown.
"I carried His mother up hill and down;
"I carried her safely to Bethlehem town,
"I," said the donkey, shaggy and brown.

"I", said the cow, all white and red,
"I gave Him my manger for His bed;
"I gave Him my hay to pillow His head;
"I said the cow, all white and red.

"I", said the sheep with curly horn,
"I gave him my wool for his blanket warm.
"He wore my coat on Christmas morn,
"I", said the sheep with curly horn.

"I", said the dove from rafters high.
"I cooed Him to sleep so He would not cry,
We cooed Him to sleep, my mate and I;
"I", said the dove from rafters high.

And every beast, by some good spell,
In the stable dark was glad to tell,
Of the gift he gave Emmanuel,
The gift he gave Emmanuel.

The Friendly Beasts

Jesus our bro-ther, strong and good, Was hum— bly born in a sta -ble rude; And the friend - ly beasts a— round Him stood, Je-sus our broth-er, strong and good.

"I", said the donkey. shaggy and brown,
"I carried His mother up hill and down;
"I carried her safely to Bethlehem town,
"I", said the donkey, shaggy and brown.

"I", said the cow, all white and red,
"I gave Him my manger for His bed;
"I gave Him my hay to pillow His head;
"I said the cow, all white and red.

"I", said the sheep with curly horn,
"I gave Him my wool for His blanket warm,
"He wore my coat on Christmas morn,
"I", said the sheep with curly horn.

"I", said the dove from rafters high,
"I cooed Him to sleep so He would not cry,
"We cooed Him to sleep, my mate and I;
"I", said the dove from rafters high.

And every beast, by some good spell,
In the stable dark was glad to tell,
Of the gift he gave Emmanuel,
The gift he gave Emmanuel.

The paintings for THE FRIENDLY BEASTS were done on 140 pound Fabriano handmade watercolor paper. The artist used transparent inks for the paintings, and handlettered the type.

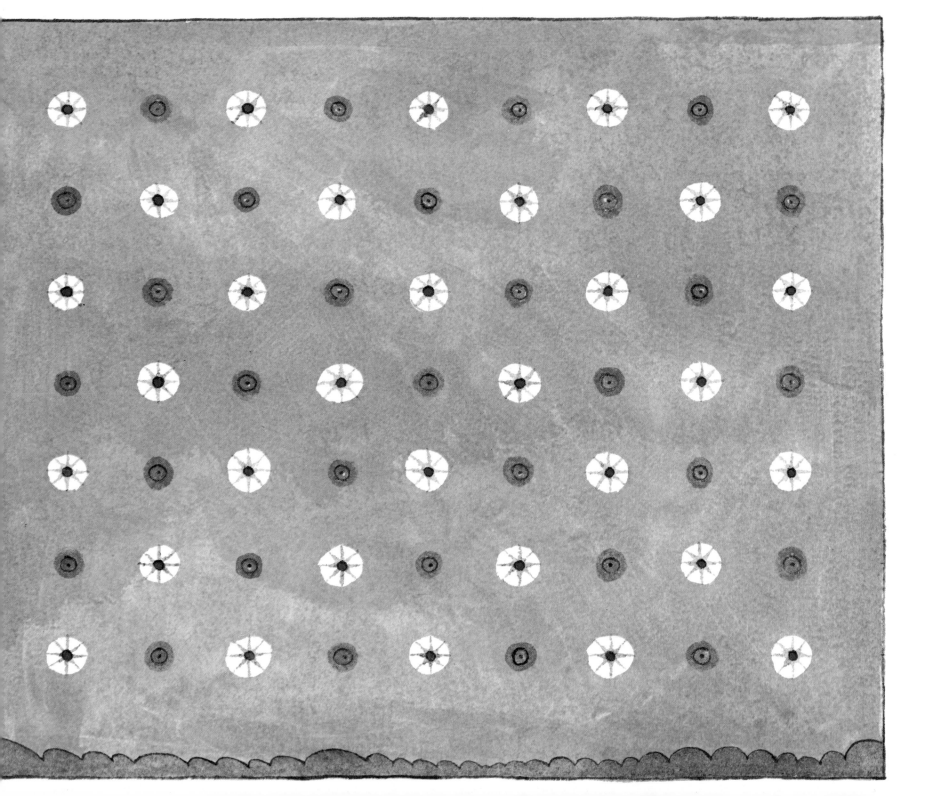